The Rooster Under the Table

a retold folktale

by Lois June Wickstrom and Jean Lorrah

All rights reserved. No part of this book may be reproduced in any form without the expressed written consent of the author and publisher.

Story © 2006, Lois June Wickstrom and Jean Lorrah

Cover ©2024 Ada Konewki

http://www.LookUnderRocks.com

The Rooster Under the Table

a retold folktale

by Lois June Wickstrom and Jean Lorrah

Once upon a time, in a land of magic, there was a princess who didn't want to marry. She wanted to have adventures, or rule a kingdom like her father. She didn't like sitting around in pretty lace-trimmed dresses, eating daintily with fancy silverware, and speaking in a soft, ladylike voice. And those were the only things a princess, or a queen, ever got to do.

Her father, the king, was an old-fashioned man. He wanted his daughter to marry. But he wasn't so old-fashioned that he would marry her to a man she didn't like. He issued a proclamation: "Any man who can win my daughter's consent to marry will earn half my kingdom now, and the rest when I die."

Soon young men lined up outside the castle for miles, all waiting to win the princess and half the kingdom. True to his generous nature, the king had hot food brought to the young men every day as they waited in line. And at night, he had warm blankets and pillows brought to them by his faithful servants. One after the other, the princess rejected each young prince when his turn came to ask her consent to marry.

After several months, the king became frustrated with all these freeloading princes who ate his food and slept in his blankets, and waited in line all day only to be rejected by his daughter. Feeding them was expensive. And they kept his servants so busy that they didn't have time to keep the castle clean.

So, the king issued a new proclamation. "Any man who can win my daughter's consent to marry will earn half my kingdom. But if he fails, he will forfeit his life."

When they heard this new announcement, most of the princes went home. Half a kingdom and a beautiful wife would be nice to have, but the chance wasn't worth having their heads chopped off.

The princess became disturbed at her father's new proclamation. She didn't want to marry, but she also didn't want to be responsible for young men having their heads chopped off.

So she took off her beautiful lace-trimmed princess dress, and put on the gardener's old muddy overalls. She stopped washing and combing her hair. She refused to take a bath. Then she squatted under the dining room table. When the young princes asked for her hand in marriage, she flapped her arms like rooster's wings and would only answer, "Aawk, Aawk."

She refused to eat anything except raw grains and bits of fruit that dropped to the floor when others ate. She became the opposite of a princess. No pretty clothes, no dainty eating, and no soft voice.

Soon word got out that the princess wasn't worth the risk of losing one's head. And the king only had to feed a prince or two each week, as they took their chances and lost. Soon the princes stopped coming altogether.

Now among the princes who had journeyed from afar was the youngest of seven sons. He was a true prince, but after his six older brothers had received their inheritance, all that was left to him was the clever rooster, Chanticleer. So he had come to court the princess in hopes of earning a kingdom of his own.

As soon as he arrived, however, he heard the news that the princess had stopped washing and combing her hair, and was living under the table, refusing to say anything but "Aawk, Aawk."

Chanticleer, the clever rooster, said, "It sounds as if she just wants to be a rooster under the table. That princess won't be marrying anyone, and you are a fool if you try to court her."

Out of money and out of luck, the young prince replied, "I must court her anyway. There are no princesses in need of rescuing from dragons or ogres, so this is my only opportunity to win a kingdom."

"But she will refuse you, and then you will just get your head cut off," said the clever rooster. "What good will that do anybody?"

"What good do I do anybody now?" asked the prince. "Without a kingdom to rule, a prince is nothing. I may as well court the princess and risk getting my head cut off."

"Wait, young sir!" said Chanticleer. "Let me go into the castle and see what the princess really wants. That may take a while, so if you want to eat in the meantime, you'd better get a job."

"A prince get a job?" exclaimed the young man in surprise.

"If a princess can be a rooster under the table, then a prince can earn his keep," said the clever rooster.

So the young prince took the only job in that kingdom available to a strong young man with no experience: helping to care for the pilgrims in the local hostelry for those who fell ill or were injured on their journey. At first he found the work hard, for he had never cared for other people in his life, but as the days passed and he saw the grateful looks on the faces of those he fed or gave water to, heard his name included in the prayers of those he lifted and cleaned after, he discovered that he liked helping others.

Meanwhile, Chanticleer flew over the castle wall and found his way into the great hall where the princess now lived under the table. She was indeed a sad sight, all dirty and unkempt, and squatting like a rooster. When he approached her, she cried "Aawk! Aawk!" and shook her arms awkwardly at him as if indeed she were trying to be a rooster under the table.

So the clever rooster ran at the princess, crying "Aawk! Aawk!" and shaking his wings at her. The princess began to imitate his movements and his squawking, becoming even more like a rooster under the table.

When people eating at the table dropped raw grains or bits of fruit, the princess and the real rooster shared them. They became roosters together under the table.

The princess and the clever rooster lived like this for several weeks, with the princess learning to act more and more like a real rooster. The king saw that his daughter was happy, so he let her and the rooster continue living under the table.

Back at the hostelry, the young prince was assigned to help the cook. The cook set him to sifting weevils out of the flour. "This is terrible!" said the prince. "Sick and injured people shouldn't have to eat bread made from flour infested with weevils!"

So he went to the clerk who did the purchasing for the hostelry, and offered to go with him to the miller on his next trip to buy flour. The prince had been trained in how to run a castle, so he knew how to bargain for the best flour at the best prices, and how to keep the miller from cheating, so they returned with clean, fresh flour that had no weevils.

"I want you to come along with me on market day!" said the clerk. Soon all their patients were eating better and getting well faster. As he watched a knight healed of a broken leg walk out the door, the young prince felt as proud as if he were ruling his own kingdom.

In the great hall of the castle that same day, somebody dropped a piece of toast under the table where the princess and the rooster were living. Chanticleer pounced on it and ate it.

The princess was shocked! "How can you eat toast, which has been cooked, if you are a rooster under the table?" she asked.

The clever rooster replied, "You've known me for months now. I am a rooster under the table, just like you. You can do anything you want to do, and still be a rooster under the table."

The princess stared at Chanticleer, realizing that a rooster had just talked to her.

Seeing her consternation, the clever rooster flapped his wings and squawked, "Aawk! Aawk!" The princess saw that he could eat toast, and he could talk—and yet he was still a rooster under the table.

Several more weeks passed, and somebody dropped a comb under the table. Chanticleer saw the princess eyeing it, and fingering her matted hair. So he began preening his feathers, as he did every day.

"Why don't you comb your hair?" he asked the princess. "You can preen your plumage and still be a rooster under the table." And he continued to smooth all his feathers into place.

The princess watched the clever rooster and thought about it. He did preen his beautiful red feathers every day, and yet he was still a rooster under the table. So she picked up the comb and began to work the knots out of her hair.

Meanwhile, the young prince was so successful at bargaining for supplies for the hostelry that the clerk in charge asked him to come along on a journey to the stone quarry, to get stone to repair the walls of the hostelry.

The journey was not long, but the return was hard, carrying the heavy slabs of stone on flatbed wagons. Therefore many men went together, among them the master mason in charge of repairs to the royal castle. He was so impressed with the bargaining abilities of the young prince that he asked him to come to the castle the next day. The master mason made plans to offer this hard-working and talented young man a position on the castle staff.

While the young prince was gone, Chanticleer noticed that the princess was more and more uncomfortable, scratching at her dirty skin. So one bright sunny afternoon he flew to the top of the courtyard fountain and proceeded to splash and bathe himself in the shallow dish there.

The princess followed the clever rooster out into the sunshine, squinting because she had not been outside in months. She stretched her body, which ached from squatting under the table and sleeping on the hard stone floor all that time, and rubbed her back as she said, "How can you go out in the sunshine and bathe in the fountain and still be a rooster under the table?"

Chanticleer flew down to the paving stones, shook the drops of water from his feathers, flapped his wings, and squawked,

"Aawk! Aawk!" Then he added, "You can do anything you want, and still be a rooster under the table." "Anything?" asked the princess. "Can I really do anything I want, and still be a rooster under the table?"

"Of course," said the rooster, flapping his wings. "Anything you want."

And now that she understood, the princess, in this land of magic, realized that the magic was within herself. First she took a bath, and then she dressed in neither the muddy overalls she had worn for months nor one of the delicate lace-trimmed dresses she despised, but in a plain loose dress that allowed her to move as she pleased. It didn't bother her in the least that people might take her for a servant. She was the only person who needed to know who she really was. Then she went in search of her father.

While she searched for the king, the princess passed through the courtyard of the castle where workmen were unloading slabs of stone to repair a tower. There she saw the clever rooster who had spent the past months with her under the table. Chanticleer perched on the wagon seat, watching as a very handsome young man discussed something with the master carpenter and the lord chamberlain.

The young man was not only handsome. Unlike all the young princes who had come courting her, his face was kind as well, and his hands were calloused from work. *That is the kind of man I want to marry,* thought the princess. *I want a partner to rule the kingdom with me, not someone who only knows how to tell other people what to do.*

And then she remembered, *I can do anything I want, and still be a rooster under the table.* So she continued in her search for her father.

When the king saw his daughter, clean and neatly dressed, out from under the table and walking like a normal person, he was so overjoyed he would have granted her anything at that moment. But the princess said to him, "Father, I have something important to tell you. The clever rooster Chanticleer has taught me that I can do anything I want, and still be a rooster under the table."

"And what do you want to do, my daughter?" asked the king.

"I want to choose my own husband. I want him to agree that he will not become king over me, but that he and I will share the kingdom together and rule jointly."

"I agree to that," said the king, "but where will you find a prince who will agree to such terms?"

"I will search until I find him," the princess replied. "But right now I must go and find the clever rooster who taught me that I can do anything I want, and still be a rooster under the table. Will you reward him, Father, with whatever he asks?"

"He's a rooster," said the king. "What could a rooster ask that I would be reluctant to grant—especially when he has given my daughter back to me? Yes, I will grant him anything he asks."

Meanwhile, the prince was eagerly telling Chanticleer what he had been doing all these weeks. "I was wrong when I said that a prince is nothing without a kingdom to rule. Helping the sick and injured to get well made me feel better than having noble blood ever did. Keeping good people from being cheated is more important than sitting on a throne. And bringing stones to repair a castle is much more satisfying than roaming around looking for dragons to kill."

Just then the princess entered the courtyard from one direction and the master mason with the lord chamberlain of the castle from the other.

"This is the young man I was telling you about," said the master mason. "He has been in our kingdom only a few months, and he has proven himself a generous and loyal subject. First he helped the sick and injured at the hostelry. Then he taught the clerk there how to bargain for the best food and not be cheated. Finally he went with us to the quarry, where he not only showed himself able to choose the best slabs of stone and not allow us to be cheated, but worked willingly with the laborers to load the stone and bring it back with us. I think you should hire him for the castle staff."

Hearing this, the princess thought, *I was right. This is definitely the kind of man I want to marry. I wonder if I can persuade my father.*

So the princess went out into the courtyard to meet the prince. As before, he took her for one of the servants, but he thought, *She is quite beautiful and seems very nice,* so he accepted the job the lord chamberlain offered him as purchasing agent, and began to flirt with the princess.

Chanticleer, the clever rooster, cocked his head to one side and decided that perhaps it was best not to tell the prince that he was courting the princess, or the princess that the man she showed such interest in was a prince.

The princess continued to dress in her plain clothes, and spent many hours with the prince, learning all the things he knew about how to run a castle in preparation for the day when she would rule the kingdom. The prince was happy to teach her, delighted to find a woman who was interested in his concerns and yet had a mind of her own.

He heard from the gossip in the castle that the princess had stopped being a rooster under the table, and was acting like a normal young woman again, but he no longer cared. He had found someone he liked better than any princess he had ever met.

The feeling was mutual, and both the prince and the princess privately confided their feelings to Chanticleer. Every once in a while, too, the princess would remind Chanticleer that her father the king had promised to reward him with anything he asked, but the clever rooster only replied, "I will wait for the day when I need a special favor from the king."

Time passed, the prince performed exceptionally as the castle's purchasing agent, and on the day when the king gave out awards for exceptional service he learned that he was to receive a small parcel of land and a portion of gold. He took the opportunity to propose marriage to the princess, whom he still thought was a servant like himself.

"I am willing to marry you," she told him, "but you know that as residents of the castle we must have the king's permission."

"I will ask him at the ceremony tomorrow," the prince replied.

The next day all the castle servants gathered in the great hall where the princess had spent so many weeks as a rooster under the table, but the only rooster under the table that day was Chanticleer.

The clever rooster stayed out of sight, watching to see what would happen. The princess was dressed as usual, in the neat plain clothes she had adopted when she had learned she could be anything she wanted to be. She looked like any of the serving women except that she was especially beautiful that day in her happiness at being in love and knowing that the man she loved - loved her in return.

The king proceeded to hand out the awards, and when it came the turn of his purchasing agent, the young prince came forward to accept the bag of gold coins and the deed to his parcel of land. Then he spoke: "Sire, I would ask another boon of you."

"And what might that be?" the king asked, a bit suspiciously.

"I ask permission to marry."

The king cheered up immediately, pleased at the sign that the bright young man would settle down. "Granted," he said. "Who is the lucky bride?"

At that, the prince held out his hand, and the princess came to his side and took it, looking adoringly into his eyes.

The king's blood pressure rose so swiftly that his face turned purple. He sputtered.

"How *dare* you?!" he demanded. "You are a servant! How dare you presume upon my kindness to court the king's own daughter?!"

And then he called his guards. "Throw him in the dungeon!" he ordered, and the prince was dragged off despite the pleadings of the princess.

"Father—you promised I could choose my own husband," the princess protested.

"This is the man I have chosen."

"I told you you could choose any *prince* you wanted," the king reminded her. "You may set your requirements, daughter, but you must also accede to mine."

The princess stood her ground. "I will go back to being a rooster under the table, Father."

"Go ahead," the king replied. "At least there you will not be destroying the royal line."

So the princess crawled back under the table with Chanticleer. As the great hall emptied in near silence, she railed at the clever rooster, "You told me I could be anything I wanted to and still be a rooster under the table. But you were wrong. I can be a rooster under the table, but I can't marry the man I love."

"Yes you can," said Chanticleer, "if the king is a man of his word as I think he is. Take me to your father, and let us see if we can work this out."

The princess stared at the clever rooster and remembered, "The promise he owes you. You are willing to use it to help me?"

"I can do anything I want, too," Chanticleer replied. "And I want to make both you and the man you love happy."

So the princess took the rooster with her and went to her father's chamber.

"Have you come to apologize?" the king asked her.

"No, Father," replied the princess. "I have come to remind you of your promise to grant Chanticleer here anything he asks of you."

The king sighed, and spoke to the clever rooster. "Yes, I do owe you, for this is the second time you have gotten my daughter out from under that table. What would you like? A golden perch? A marble chicken coop with ten beautiful hens to be your harem? Tell me, and it's yours." "Anything I ask?" asked Chanticleer.

"That was my promise," the king replied.

"Then I ask that you permit the marriage between your daughter and the man she loves."

"No," said the king. "He is a commoner and a servant. He cannot marry a princess."

"He can be a prince if you say the word," replied Chanticleer. "He can do whatever he wants, just as your daughter can do whatever *she* wants."

The king looked at his daughter. "Do you really want to be a rooster under the table again, squatting there all dirty and going 'Aawk, aawk' at everyone who tries to talk to you?"

"No," replied the princess. "I want to marry the man I love. If he can't be a prince, then I will be a commoner. Keep your promise to Chanticleer: permit the marriage, and my husband and I will go away and earn our living in another kingdom."

Then she smiled at Chanticleer and said, "You see? I have learned what you taught me. I really can do anything I want and still be a rooster under the table."

"I could permit the marriage," said the king, "and then immediately after the ceremony have the groom's head cut off."

"And I," replied the princess, "could then end my days as a grieving widow, never marrying anyone, and leaving your kingdom with no heir, ever."

The king sighed, knowing he was defeated now that his daughter truly understood that she could do whatever she wanted, one way or another. "Very well, my stubborn rooster under the table," he replied, "you may marry the man you love, if he will agree to your terms."

The prince was only too happy to agree, for he had already discovered how much fun it was to run a castle together—so why not a kingdom?

There was a magnificent wedding, and all the people cheered to see their princess married to a kind and clever man. The prince never did tell anyone that he was a prince, as it no longer mattered—everyone in the kingdom learned the story and the lesson, "You can do anything you want, and still be a rooster under the table."

And every once in a while, the prince and the princess joined Chanticleer under the table, stuck out their elbows and shouted "Aawk Aawk," just because they could still do anything they wanted and still be roosters under the table.

www.ingramcontent.com/pod-product-compliance
Lightning Source LLC
LaVergne TN
LVHW061044070526
838201LV00073B/5167